'Luv'
Renée Suchmiecky

written by Renee Pendleton Suchowiecky, M.Ed.
illustrated by Jodi Gold

Gi Gi & Tots Books

Lollipup and Luvable are best of friends.
Each day they meet
where the country road bends.

Lollipup's knapsack,
  purple and teal,
Luvable, loving
  as her heart is real.

"Dynamo duo! Talented two!
Together there's nothing
we cannot do.
With sunbeams of yellow,
let's fill the air.
With 'do-good' hearts,
we're a perfect pair."

Then in a flash, they make a dash.
They run so fast, they almost crash!
Through the meadow, up the hill,
Bound to see their good friend Will.

Will lies sick with an aching belly,
From fourteen pickles he ate at the deli.
From the knapsack, they pull out gifts,
Three yellow daffodils and one gold fish.

Lollipup and Luvable
dash out the door,
Heading straight
for the candy store.

They find
fallen Frankie,
flat on the floor.
And hand him
a hanky saying,
"Cry no more."

With Frankie teary
and still a bit weary,
What in the world can make him cheery?
Doggy bones and lollipops,
green, red and blue,

A little bit of music
and boogie-woogie too.

The 'do-good' dogs
are ready to snack,
So they pull out cookies
from the purple knapsack.

Two hungry ants crawling,
plus one in the tree,
The dogs then decide,
"Let's share with all three!"

"Janie and Mamie won't let me play."
Lollipup says, "They can't
treat you that way.
Be confident and caring
and treat others well.
Then friends will flock to you,
this I can tell."

Lollipup demands, "Stop this minute."
Luvable adds, "No one can win it.

Looks a lot like this day is done.
We helped our friends and had some fun.

"Dynamo duo! Talented two!
Together there's nothing we cannot do!"

Find a do-good deed and match it with its picture.

1. Be good to your Mom & Dad.
2. Help those who are hurt.
3. Be a kind friend.
4. Bring cheer to the sick.
5. Make peace between people who quarrel.
6. Share with others.

_____

_____

_____

_____

_____

_____